Hello, Family Members,

Learning to read is one of the most important accomplishments of early childhood. **Hello Reader!** books are designed to help children become skilled readers who like to read. Beginning readers learn to read by remembering frequently used words like "the," "is," and "and"; by using phonics skills to decode new words; and by interpreting picture and text clues. These books provide both the stories children enjoy and the structure they need to read fluently and independently. Here are suggestions for helping your child *before*, *during*, and *after* reading:

Before

- Look at the cover and pictures and have your child predict what the story is about.
- Read the story to your child.
- Encourage your child to chime in with familiar words and phrases.
- Echo read with your child by reading a line first and having your child read it after you do.

During

- Have your child think about a word he or she does not recognize right away. Provide hints such as "Let's see if we know the sounds" and "Have we read other words like this one?"
- Encourage your child to use phonics skills to sound out new words.
- Provide the word for your child when more assistance is needed so that he or she does not struggle and the experience of reading with you is a positive one.
- Encourage your child to have fun by reading with a lot of expression . . . like an actor!

After

- Have your child keep lists of interesting and favorite words.
- Encourage your child to read the books over and over again. Have him or her read to brothers, sisters, grandparents, and even teddy bears. Repeated readings develop confidence in young readers.
- Talk about the stories. Ask and answer questions. Share ideas about the funniest and most interesting characters and events in the stories.

I do hope that you and your child enjoy this book.

—Francie Alexander
Reading Specialist,
Scholastic's Instructional Publishing Group

For Billy and Rob
—A. M. B.

For Carolyn, Bill, Alex, Nick, and Lilli
—L. D. F.

Text copyright © 1998 by Adele M. Brodkin.
Illustrations copyright © 1998 by Larry Di Fiori.
All rights reserved. Published by Scholastic Inc.
SCHOLASTIC, HELLO READER! and CARTWHEEL BOOKS
and associated logos are trademarks and/or registered
trademarks of Scholastic Inc.

Library of Congress Cataloging-in-Publication Data

Brodkin, Adele M.
  The lonely only dog / by Adele M. Brodkin; illustrated by Larry Di
Fiori.
    p.   cm. — (Hello reader! Level 3)
  "Cartwheel books."
  Summary: A dog who longs for someone to play with finds out how
good life is as an only pet when another dog comes to visit.

  ISBN 0-590-52280-9

  [1. Dogs—Fiction.   2. Loneliness—Fiction.   3. Only child—fiction.]
I. Di Fiori, Lawrence, ill.   II. Title.   III. Series.
PZ7.B786116Lo   1998
[E] — dc21   97-7782
                                                    CIP
                                                    AC

12 11 10 9 8 7 6 5 4 3 2 1   8 9/9 0/0 01 02 03
                    Printed in the U.S.A.   24
                First printing, November 1998

The Lonely Only Dog

by Adele M. Brodkin • Illustrated by Larry Di Fiori

Hello Reader! — Level 3

SCHOLASTIC INC. Cartwheel B·O·O·K·S ®

New York Toronto London Auckland Sydney

Harry was a happy dog. He had everything a dog could want.
In the kitchen, he had a big, soft pillow—just for him. He had a bowl of fresh food—just for him.

Harry had bowls of water—upstairs and downstairs. He had toys and bones and pillows everywhere—just for him.

Harry got a treat every time he would sit, lie down, or roll over. He even got a treat when he barked at the closet where the treats were kept.

Harry loved tricks and games. Every
night, Gwen and Greg walked to the
stairs. Harry ran ahead with his
orange ball.

Harry let the ball bounce down — one step
at a time. Gwen and Greg tossed it back up.
"One, two, three, give!" they shouted.
Then the game began again.

Harry, Gwen, and Greg walked
in the park. There was much to
sniff and see and hear.

Sometimes they took long walks
in the woods. Then Harry would
be glad to go home to his bones
and pillows and treats.

One day, Harry, Gwen, and Greg walked in front of a pet shop window. Some puppies were snoozing and snuggling. Others were wrestling. For the first time, Harry felt like a lonely only dog. He wanted to snuggle and wrestle, too.

Then, Harry, Gwen, and Greg saw some
dogs walking together. One dog nipped.
Two dogs nuzzled. Harry wished he
could be one of them.

In the park, Harry saw dogs in packs or pairs. He wondered why his family only had him. Why was he a lonely dog?

That night, Harry felt sad. Gwen and
Greg were at the movies. Harry tried
dozing on one of his pillows. But it
wasn't any fun.

He tried chewing a bone. But it wasn't any fun. Harry wanted to play dog tug-of-war or chase a friend around the couch. He was a lonely only dog.

That night, Harry did not drop his orange ball on the steps. He stayed curled up in a corner.

Gwen and Greg were worried, but the vet
said Harry wasn't sick.

No one knew what was wrong. Then Gwen had an idea. "Harry needs another dog to play with," she said. So Gwen and Greg asked two friends from far away to visit with their dog, Arthur.

Harry wagged his tail. He was happy to have a new friend.

Harry and Arthur chased each other.

They ate from each other's bowls.
They curled up together and slept.
It was a great day.

But the next morning, Arthur
took Harry's favorite bone.

Harry saw that his food bowl was empty.
His water bowl was empty, too.

That night, Arthur grabbed Harry's orange ball. Gwen and Greg called out, "One, two, three, give!" They were playing *his* game with Arthur!

Harry did something he had never done
before. He growled and showed his teeth.
Greg scolded. Harry crept into a corner
while Arthur curled up on Harry's big, soft
pillow for the night.

The next morning everyone went for a walk.
Arthur wanted to race, but Harry did not.
Harry stayed with Gwen and Greg. They
were *his* people. This was *his* walk in *his*
park. Harry longed to be an only dog again.

Finally, the day came for Arthur
to go home. Harry howled for joy.

Inside, Harry ran around and around. He greeted his own things. He drank his own water. He ate his own food. He ran up and down the stairs with his own orange ball.

Then Harry curled up on his big, soft pillow. Harry was still an only dog—but he knew he would never be lonely again!